Weekly Reader Children's Book Club presents

# The Thief
## in the
# Botanical Gardens

*Diane Redfield Massie*

Xerox Education Publications

XEROX

Publishing, Executive, and Editorial Offices:
Xerox Education Publications
Middletown, Connecticut 06457

ISBN 0-88375-207-7

Library of Congress Catalogue Card Number: 74-22655

Weekly Reader Children's Book Club Edition
XEROX® is a trademark of Xerox Corporation.

*for Maud*

R abbit had a brand new job.
"I'm keeper of the Botanical Gardens!" he said,
waving to his friends. "Look at my new blue coat."
"Wow!" said Turtle. "It's got gold buttons."

Rabbit put it on. "I'm going to live in the keeper's cottage," he said. "My things are all moved in!" He rang the new bell, hanging from his doorknocker.

"Gee," said the crows.

"I've got shovels and rakes and clippers and things,"
said Rabbit, hopping on one foot.

"Let's see," said Possum.

Rabbit brought everything out of the shed and laid it
on the path.

"Can I try the clippers?" asked Frog.

"No!" said Rabbit. "Only the keeper can use them."

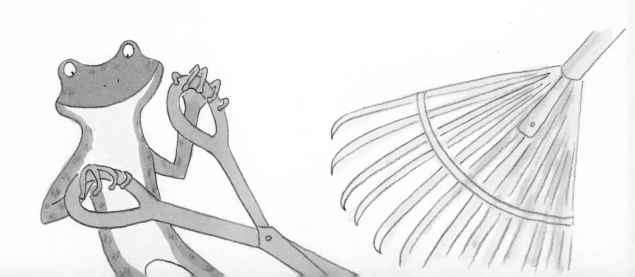

The crows flew over the zinnia beds and landed
in the grass.

"Keep off the grass," said Rabbit.

"But, Rabbit," said the crows, "we're looking
for worms like we always do."

"Botanical gardens have rules," said Rabbit,
picking up his tools. "I'll be putting up some signs."

"What signs?" asked Turtle.

Rabbit went inside his keeper's cottage and shut the door.

"Well!" said the crows. "What do you make of *that*?"

"Who knows?" said Turtle.

"And anyway," said Rabbit, looking out the window, "when I was hired, I had to repeat *The Keeper's Motto*!"

"What's that?" asked Possum.

"*Be friendly, firm, and on the job*!" He shut the window.

"He's certainly firm and on the job," said Turtle.

"What happened to *friendly*?" said Frog.

Rabbit was up early next morning, putting up signs in the garden. "Keepers have got to be firm," he said. "No swimming! No climbing! No picnicking! No sleeping! No . . . "

"Rabbit!" called his friends outside the gate. "Let us in."

"Keep off the grass!" said Rabbit to himself, "and no picking flowers!" He crossed the path and opened the big front gate.

"Did you say something about flowers?" asked Turtle. "They *do* look delicious."

"*Delicious*?" said Rabbit. "Flowers are to be admired, not eaten!" He straightened his coat and glared at Turtle.

"I was only kidding," said Turtle. He crawled under the begonias and settled down for his nap.

The crows flew, cawing, over the trees and landed in the grass.

SPLASH! went Frog in the fountain. He swam about, snapping at gnats.

And Possum climbed up in the tulip tree with her babies on her back.

"STOP!" shouted Rabbit,
hopping up and down.
"What are you doing?"

"Just what we always do,"
said his friends,
looking at each other.

"Can't you *read*?" said Rabbit.

"Read?" said Frog.

"The signs!" said Rabbit. He hopped about, pointing at signs.
"NO SWIMMING! NO CLIMBING! NO SLEEPING!
And KEEP OFF THE GRASS!"

"Shhhhhh!" whispered Possum. "You'll wake up my babies."

"We're finding worms," said the crows.

"I'm catching gnats," said Frog.

"And *I*," said Turtle, "am trying to take a nap." He blinked his yellow eyes.

"Then you'll all have to leave," said Rabbit,
"until you learn to obey the rules."

"Leave?" said everyone.

Possum crawled down the tree. Her babies hung onto
her fur. "What *can* one do in the Botanical Gardens?"
she said, sniffing crossly. "We're going home!"

Rabbit finished his breakfast the next morning
and hurried out to unlock the gate.

"Good morning," called the crows, flying through the
trees.

"Good morning," said Turtle. "I was the first one here—
even before the crows."

Possum's babies scampered down the path.

"Wait for Mommy," said Possum.

"Hi!" croaked Frog, heading for the fountain.

"Keep off the grass!" called Rabbit, "and don't pick the . . . GOOD HEAVENS!" He stopped and stared at the lily beds. "WHAT'S HAPPENED TO THE LILIES?"

The tiger lilies were bitten off. Only their leaves
were left.

"SOMEONE'S EATEN THE LILIES!" shouted Rabbit,
stumbling over the hose.

"Well," said Turtle, "it wasn't *me*."

"Maybe it was!" said Rabbit. "Or maybe it was Frog!"
He examined the bitten stems.

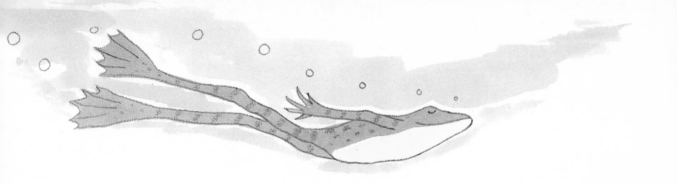

"Frogs eat gnats," said Frog, leaping into the fountain.
He swam under water around the side.

"It must have been the crows!" said Rabbit.

The crows were busy getting worms in the grass.

"Or maybe the possums ate them!" Rabbit ran home again,
and made a large sign: DO NOT EAT THE LILIES! He put the
sign next to the lily beds. *"No eating tiger lilies in the
Botanical Gardens!"* he yelled.

Turtle was asleep under the begonias.

Possum swung gently in the tulip tree. Her babies' eyes were closed.

"Caw Caw Caw," said the crows in the grass.

And Frog floated dreamily under the fountain.

"Dear me!" sighed Rabbit. "How tiring it is to be keeper of the Botanical Gardens!" He locked the gate early that evening and went home.

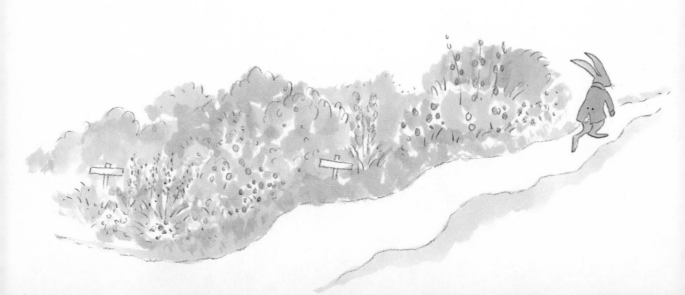

Turtle was waiting at the gate the next morning
when Rabbit came down the path.

"Where are the begonias?"
asked Turtle.

"The begonias?" said Rabbit,
undoing the lock.
"Looks like they've been
eaten," said Turtle.

"That settles it!" said Rabbit. "THE BOTANICAL GARDENS
ARE CLOSED!" He slammed the gate in Turtle's face
and locked the lock again.

"But *I* didn't eat them," said Turtle.

"I'M GOING TO FIND OUT WHO DID!" shouted Rabbit.
"It was either you, or frog, or the crows, or the possums!
You're all under suspicion!" And he stamped down the path.

Possum came hurrying up with her babies. "Isn't the gate open yet?" she asked.

"No," said Turtle. "It's closed today. Someone ate the begonias."

Rabbit took out his flashlight. He waited until it
was dark. "I'll catch that thief," he said, "if it takes me
all night!" He hurried down the path in the moonlight and
hid among the rose bushes.

The big white moon moved slowly up over the poplar trees.
The garden was still.

"Threereee! Threeeereee threeeeeree!"

"STOP THIEF!" yelled Rabbit, leaping out of the bushes.
His flashlight fell to the ground.

"Thief?" said a cricket, whirring his wings.
"Oh," said Rabbit. "It was only you."

"*I'm* no thief," said the cricket, crossly. "You'd better
watch your language!" And he hopped away in the dark.

Rabbit sat down in the grass. His jacket was damp with
dew. "It's cold out here," he said, rubbing his tired eyes.
He leaned against a peony bush and listened to the locusts
singing like bees in the night. Soon he was fast asleep.
He slept until morning.

"Rabbit!" called Turtle through the gate. "Wake up!"

"What?" said Rabbit, leaping in the air. "STOP THIEF!"

"Thief?" said Turtle. "Where?"

"So I've caught you, Turtle!" said Rabbit. "It was you all along!" He rubbed his eyes with his paws.

"Me?" said Turtle. "I just got here."

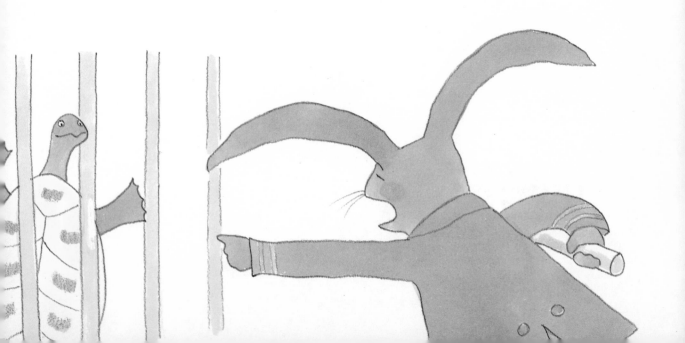

"I knew you'd come out tonight," said Rabbit, waving his flashlight in the air.

"But, Rabbit," said Turtle, "it's morning."

"Oh," said Rabbit, looking about. "So it is."

"It's nine o'clock," said Turtle. "Time to open the gate."

"The gate will remain closed," shouted Rabbit, "until the thief is caught!" He went inside his cottage and slammed the door.

As soon as the sun went down that evening, Rabbit took out his camera. He fastened a flashbulb on top. Then he found a piece of string in his drawer and hurried off through the garden. "Ah!" said Rabbit, stopping next to the zinnia beds. He set up his camera in the grass, tying one end of the string to the shutter and the other to the largest zinnia he could find. "There!" he said, clapping his paws. "Tonight, when someone comes to eat the zinnias, he'll pull on the string and the camera will take his picture. And *then* we'll know who the flower thief is!"

That night he dreamed of zinnias blooming in the
moonlight. He slept until dawn.

"I must get up!" said Rabbit, pulling on his coat.
He ran down the path in the early morning light
and pushed through the zinnia plants. "Ah ha!" said Rabbit.
"Just as I thought! The zinnias are gone!" He hurriedly
wound up the string and carried his camera out the gate,
down to the camera shop.

"Open up!" called Rabbit, pounding on the door.

"What?" said Weasel, looking down from his window.
He rubbed his eyes and yawned.

"Open up in the name of the Botanical Gardens!"
said Rabbit.

"The what?" said Weasel.

"I've got the thief's picture!" said Rabbit,
patting his camera.

"Thief?" said Weasel.

"Come down!" said Rabbit. "We haven't time to talk."
Weasel shut the window.

Rabbit waited while Weasel found his slippers and robe. At last he unlocked the door.

"I've got the thief!" said Rabbit again, swinging his camera in the air. "Right here in this box!"

"In there?" said Weasel.

Rabbit pushed his way inside. He took out the roll of film. "Can you develop it right now?" he asked.

"I haven't had breakfast yet," said Weasel.

"BREAKFAST?" Rabbit shouted. "Breakfast would obstruct the law!" he cried. "The Botanical Gardens has a thief and he must be caught at once!"

"Oh," said Weasel, "in that case . . . " He took the roll into his darkroom.

Rabbit walked up and down. "It was probably Turtle who ate them," he said to himself. "Or maybe it was Frog . . . Then again," he said aloud, "the crows were . . . "

"Here it is," said Weasel.

Rabbit snatched the picture out of his paws. He stared with his mouth open wide. "It's a picture of *me!*" he said. He sat down on the bench and stared at himself standing among the zinnias. "It *can't* be *me!*" said Rabbit.

"It looks like you," said Weasel, yawning. "That will be fifty-three cents, please. You can put it on the counter. I'm going back to bed." He yawned again and climbed the stairs behind the storeroom curtain.

Rabbit dropped the money on the counter and went slowly out the door. He climbed the hill to the Botanical Gardens. Turtle was already waiting at the gate.

"What are you doing out *here*?" asked Turtle. "Why aren't you inside?"

"Look," said Rabbit, holding out the picture. "Who does this look like?"

"It's you," said Turtle.

"Are you sure?" Rabbit sat down at the side of the gate. He told Turtle about the camera in the grass, and the string to the zinnias across the path, and how he was home all the while asleep in bed.

"Sounds like you were sleepwalking, to *me*," said Turtle. "And you ate the flowers yourself."

"Do you mean . . . " said Rabbit, "that I'm . . . " Tears filled his eyes.

"You're the flower thief," said Turtle.

"Oh, *no!*" cried Rabbit. He fell in the dirt and lay
on his back. Tears rolled down his whiskers. He covered
his eyes with his paws.

"You didn't *mean* to eat them," said Turtle.
"You were asleep."

"What's the matter?" called the crows, flying
over the gate.

Turtle waved them on. "Nothing," he said.

Rabbit got up. He unlocked the gate with his key. "I can't be the keeper now," he said. "I'm not fit to be keeper anymore." Tears rolled down his nose. "Turtle," he said sadly, "you'll have to be the new keeper." He took off his coat and gave it to Turtle.

"I don't want to be keeper," said Turtle. "I like to *sleep* half the day." He looked hopefully at the begonia bushes. "And anyway," said Turtle, holding out the coat, "you'd be all right as keeper if you just weren't so cross."

"Keepers *have* to be cross," said Rabbit, wiping his nose on his arm. "They have to be *awfully* cross because of all the rules. No picking! No climbing! No swimming! No eating! Rules like that," said Rabbit.

"Who *made* the rules?" asked Turtle.

"*I* did," said Rabbit.

Turtle smiled. "Maybe you made too *many* rules," he said.

They sat down together and watched the birds fly high in the sky, dipping and turning above the poplar trees.

"How did *The Keeper's Motto* go again?" asked Turtle.

Rabbit shuffled his feet. "*Be friendly, be firm . . .*"

"Ah, that's it!" said Turtle. "Be *friendly*." He looked at Rabbit. "Maybe that's the most *important* part of being keeper," he said.

"Maybe," said Rabbit.

They sat awhile, watching the clouds.

"Turtle," sighed Rabbit,
"*how* will I stop eating flowers?"

Turtle thought a moment.
"*I* know!" he said, jumping up.
"You can tie a bell on the end
of your foot at night!"
"What for?" sighed Rabbit.

"The bell will ring if you get out of bed and wake you
up," said Turtle. "And then you can go back to bed again!"
"WOW!" cried Rabbit, grabbing his coat. He turned a
somersault in the air and landed on his feet. "Lucky for
me, I *have* a bell!" he said, running up the path to his door.

"I'M KEEPER OF THE BOTANICAL GARDENS!" he yelled, "AND
I WON'T EAT THE FLOWERS ANYMORE!" He went inside.

When the sun rose in the morning, Rabbit was busy at work. "Good morning," said Turtle, crawling through the gate. "I see the gardens are blooming."

Rabbit smiled with pride.

"Hi," croaked Frog, jumping over the stones. He leaped, with a splash, into the fountain.

The crows were stepping about in the grass. "We're hunting for worms," they said.

"What are *you* doing?" asked Possum, climbing up the tree.

"I'm taking down the signs," said Rabbit. "It's nicer here without them."

"HOORAY!" yelled Frog.

"WOW!" cried the crows.

"Shhhh!" whispered Possum. "You'll wake my babies."

Turtle crawled under a begonia bush.

"*Thank you*, Turtle," said Rabbit, smelling a marigold.

"And have a nice nap," he said.